THE OFFICE FRO

BY **DON SMITH**

POWERFRESH

Under license from CCC Publications, California, USA.

Published in the UK by
POWERFRESH Limited
3 Gray Street
Northampton
NN1 3QQ

Telephone 44 01604 30996
Facsimile 44 01604 21013

Under License from CCC Publications
California, USA

Cover and interior illustration CCC Publications

Cover Graphics and interior layout Powerfresh

THE OFFICE FROM HELL
ISBN 1 874125 34 1

Printed in the UK by Avalon Print Northampton
Powerfresh August 1994

THE OFFICE FROM HELL

INTRODUCTION

THE OFFICE FROM HELL PROBABLY NEEDS NO INTRODUCTION BECAUSE ANYONE WHO HAS EVER WORKED IN AN OFFICE ANY TIME, ANYWHERE, WILL RECOGNISE CO-WORKERS AND BOSSES WHO SEEM TO HAVE COME FROM SOME EPISODE OF THE ''TWILIGHT ZONE.'' A FEW UNLUCKY SOULS LIVE IN THE OFFICE FROM HELL DAY IN AND DAY OUT... BUT EVEN THE BEST OFFICE HAS ITS HELLISH DAYS. SO DESCEND WITH US NOW TO THE SIXTH RING OF ''THE INFERNO,'' ESPECIALLY DESIGNATED FOR THOSE NERDS, DWEEBS AND FIENDS WHO SOMETIMES MAKE YOUR LIFE A NIGHTMARE. YOU'LL SEE MANY FAMILIAR FACES AND IF YOU LOOK CLOSELY, WHO KNOWS, YOU MIGHT EVEN FIND YOURSELF!

GEE ! A
TYPEWRITER
WITH A
TV SCREEN!
CAN I WATCH
``NEIGHBOURS''
ON IT?

YOUR COMPUTER
WAS FULL..

SO I EMPTIED IT.

CAN SOMEBODY
TAKE THE PHONE CALLS
FOR AN HOUR ?

I GOTTA TYPE A LETTER

CAN I
GET
WORKERS
COMPENSATION
FOR A
BROKEN
FINGERNAIL ?

I HOPE
THIS ISN'T
ONE OF
THOSE OFFICES
WHERE THERE'S
A LOT
OF PRESSURE
TO BE
GOOD.

I SHOULDA
BEEN HERE
AT NINE ?
WHY ? DID
I MISS
SOMETHING ?

NOW, BEFORE
I TELL YOU
WHAT I
DID, YOU
HAVE TO
PROMISE
YOU WON'T
GET MAD.

THOSE LITTLE
COLOURED TABS
WERE
CLASHING !
SO I MOVED ALL THE
FILES AROUND
AND NOW THEY'RE
COLOUR
COORDINATED
AND THEY LOOK
LOVELY !

YOU WANT SOMEONE
WHO CAN **TYPE !!** OH!
I THOUGHT YOU JUST WANTED
SOMEONE WHO WAS **FAST** !

YOU KNOW WHAT
THEY SAY -
ALL WORK
AND NO PLAY !

DON'T WORRY
ABOUT ME..
I MARCH TO
A DIFFERENT
DRUMMER

OF COURSE
YOU DON'T
HAVE TO
WAIT **ALL**
DAY !!
WE
CLOSE
AT 5 !

AFTER YOU'VE BEEN
HERE A WHILE YOU
REALISE THAT BENEATH
THAT GRUFF EXTERIOR LIES
A HEART OF SOLID
 GRANITE.

THIS IS
BILL'S MOTHER.
I KNOW HE'S
SUPPOSED TO
BE THERE AT 9
BUT HE GOT IN
LATE LAST NIGHT
AND I JUST
HATE TO WAKE
HIM UP.

I REALLY NEEDED
THIS JOB ...
I HAVEN'T BEEN ABLE
TO GET ANYTHING
SINCE I SUED
MY LAST BOSS

HEY,
WHERE'S
THE BROOM?
I NEED TO
FINISH
PUTTIN' THE
VAN IN
THE GARAGE

DO YOU
WANT
THE BOSS
OR SOMEONE
WHO KNOWS
WHAT HE'S
TALKING ABOUT ?

DEAR MUM,
I WISH MIZ
RATZBURGER,
MY 3RD YEAR
ENGLISH TICHER
CUD SEE ME NOW.
SHE SED I'D
NEVER GET
ENNYWHERE !
BUT HEER
I ARE, A
SEKRYTERRY

THE
LAST PLACE
I WORKED
I WAS
THE
LOOKOUT

OF COURSE I'M
RESPONSIBLE !
ON MY LAST JOB
THEY BLAMED ME
FOR EVERYTHING !

OK! SO
WHICH WAY
IS THE
SECRETARIAL POOL?

THEY
MADE ME
ROUTING
SUPERVISOR
BECAUSE I LIKE
TELLIN' PEOPLE
WHERE TO GO

FIRST
THINGS
FIRST.
WHERE'S
THE
MICROWAVE?

THERE'S A MR COOK
OUT HERE WITH A TV CREW.
I TOLD HIM YOU WERE IN.

YOU NEED
SOMEBODY
FOR A HIGH
LEVEL
POSITION ?

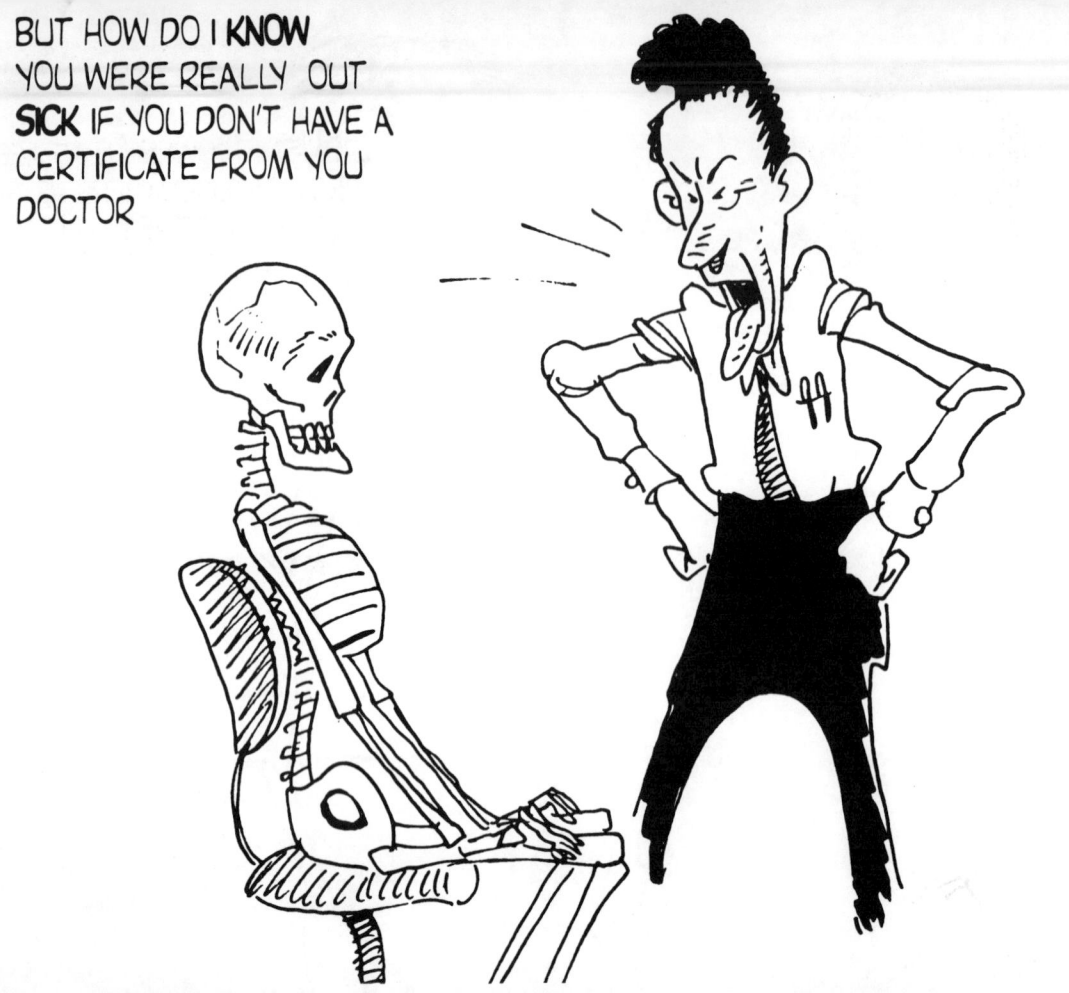

ABOUT THE "AUTHOR"

DON SMITH OWNS AN AD AGENCY AND DESIGN STUDIO WHERE HE MET MANY OF THE CHARACTERS IN THIS BOOK.. HIS HUMOUROUS ILLUSTRATIONS HAVE BEEN USED ON BILLBOARDS, RECORD JACKETS, PACKAGES, ADVERTISING AND IN BOOKS. DON ALSO HAS A LONG-RUNNING CARTOON CALLED, "IT'S A WEIRD WORLD," WHICH APPEARS IN HIS LOCAL PAPER.

"WE ALL BELIEVE EVERYONE IN THE WORLD, (EXCEPT US) IS WEIRD..." SAYS SMITH, "SO IT DOESN'T TAKE MUCH EXAGGERATION ON MY PART TO CURRICULATE THE PEOPLE I OBSERVE."

MAYBE YOU CAN SLEEP BETTER AT NIGHT KNOWING THAT DON IS KEEPING AN EYE OUT FOR THE WEIRDOS. OR MAYBE NOT.

TITLES BY

POWERFRESH

CRINKLED 'N' WRINKLED
DRIVEN CRAZY
OH NO ITS XMAS AGAIN
TRUE LOVE
IT'S A BOY
IT'S A GIRL
NOW WE ARE 40
FUNNY SIDE OF 40 HIM
FUNNY SIDE OF 40 HER
FUNNY SIDE OF 50 HIM
FUNNY SIDE OF 50 HER
FUNNY SIDE OF GOLF
FUNNY SIDE OF 60'S
FUNNY SIDE OF SEX
GERRY ATTRIC'S GAG BOOK
THE COMPLETE WIMPS GUIDE TO SEX
THE COMPLETE BASTARDS GUIDE TO BUSINESS SURVIVAL
THE COMPLETE BASTARDS GUIDE TO SPORT
THE COMPLETE BASTARDS GUIDE TO LIFE
THE COMPLETE BASTARDS GUIDE TO SEX
MALCOM
KEEP FIT WITH YOUR CAT
THE OFFICE FROM HELL
MONSTERS
MARITAL BLISS AND OTHER OXYMORONS
THE ART OF SLOBOLOGY

ALL TITLES RETAIL AT   £2.99